Tadpoles

Sammy's Secret

by Margaret Nash

Illustrated by Anni Axworthy

W

FRANKLIN WATTS

LONDON•SYDNEY

Margaret Nash

"I think all cats have secrets. I'm sure my cat Tabitha has. But I know she hasn't got one like Sammy's!"

Anni Axworthy

"My two dogs were very unhappy about me painting all these cats, but I had a good time!"

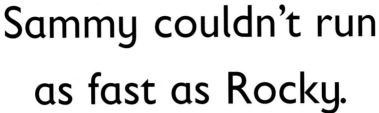

Sammy couldn't run
as fast as Rocky.

Sammy couldn't jump
as high as Jess.

Sammy couldn't climb
as far as Kitty.

"You're too small,"
they said.

10

Rocky

"You need to grow!"

So Sammy hung
from the door.

He stretched out
on the floor.

He rolled up in a ball.

But he was still small.

"There is something
I *can* do," said Sammy.

ROCKY

KITTY

19

And one day, when
the rain beat down ...

... he did it!

"Miaow! Miaow!"

Sammy

23

Notes for adults

TADPOLES is structured to provide support for newly independent readers. The stories may also be used by adults for sharing with young children.

Starting to read alone can be daunting. **TADPOLES** helps by providing visual support and repeating words and phrases. These books will both develop confidence and encourage reading and rereading for pleasure.

If you are reading this book with a child, here are a few suggestions:

1. Make reading fun! Choose a time to read when you and the child are relaxed and have time to share the story.

2. Talk about the story before you start reading. Look at the cover and the blurb. What might the story be about? Why might the child like it?

3. Encourage the child to reread the story, and to retell the story in their own words, using the illustrations to remind them what has happened.

4. Discuss the story and see if the child can relate it to their own experience, or perhaps compare it to another story they know.

5. Give praise! Remember that small mistakes need not always be corrected.

If you enjoyed this book, why not try another **TADPOLES** story?